SYLVESTER & TWEETY

READ THE MYSTERY

Fangs for the Memories

Bath New York Singapore Hong Kong Cologne Delhi Melbourne

Story by Sid Jacobson
Pencils by Pablo Zamboni and Walter Carzon
Inks by Duendes del Sur
Color by Barry Grossman

First published by Parragon in 2008
Parragon
Queen Street House
4 Queen Street
Bath BA1 1HE, UK

PARR 8201

ISBN 978-1-4075-2630-0

Printed in USA

Granny and her two pets, Tweety and Sylvester, were driving through the Transylvanian countryside.

"As you might know," she said to Tweety and Sylvester, "this is vampire land. And vampires are supposed to thrive on the blood of others." Sylvester shrieked with fear.

"Oh, Sylvester," laughed Granny. "It's all a make believe story. For all the tales of Count Dracula, no vampire like that has ever existed. Even in Transylvania."

"Don't you wead?" said Tweety. He had heard about the real count known as Dracula, and he was a very bad man who had lived in this area, but he was not a vampire.

The sky darkened with black clouds and the thunder roared. It grew worse as rain poured down and fog appeared.

"We'd better find shelter," said Granny.

"So long as it isn't Dracula's castle," thought Sylvester with a shiver. It wasn't, but it was something awfully close.

"Let's drive up to that big house," said Granny, turning into the driveway of a large, castle-like structure.

"I d-don't l-like this," stammered Sylvester.

"We'll be just fine, scaredy tat," Tweety answered, as they jumped out of the car and ran toward the house.

Granny knocked on the large door of the house. A man with a skull-like face and a butler's uniform answered.

"You poor things," he said sadly, looking at the three drenched figures. "Please come in. The count will be with you shortly."

"Please don't say it's Count Dracula," thought Sylvester.

In moments, the count entered and bowed before them.
"Welcome to my humble home," he said. "I am Count Crackula!"
"Oh, no," thought Sylvester.
"He said Crackula," Tweety whispered. "Not Dracula."

Granny looked around the huge castle room. It was as high as a tall tree and big enough to hold three staircases.

"Cozy, isn't it?" said the count. Only Igor and myself live here, so we like visitors. Especially since I sleep all day."

Tweety gulped. "Like a vampire," he thought.

"And now, I must go upstairs to watch my favorite TV show, The Vampire Game," The count smiled, revealing two sharp teeth, like the fangs of a VAMPIRE!

"Igor will bring you as much food as you like," he added, "and show you where to sleep."

The servant, Igor, arrived carrying a large platter of food. "This should feed you all," he said, placing it on a coffee table. He pointed to a large sofa at the side. "It pulls out into a bed," he added. "And pay no attention to the noises. We believe someone lost a radio here that we still can't find."

"What kind of a place is this?" Granny said, aloud. "The count has fangs, sleeps all day and watches The Vampire Game, while Igor talks about noises. They act as if a real vampire lives here."

"I told you so!" Sylvester whispered to Tweety.

After dinner, Granny pulled open the sofa bed.
Granny tried to stay awake to make sure everyone
was safe, but she fell fast asleep in minutes. And ten
minutes later, the two pets began to hear noises.

"Did you h-hear th-that?" Sylvester stammered. "That sounded like someone moaning!"

SHRIEK! Another sound from the far end of the large room.

"Either this is the house of a vampire," said Tweety, "or someone is twying to scare us!"

"And I don't believe in vampires," he said, getting up.

The moaning went on as Tweety moved about the large room. First, it came from one side, then from another.

"If that comes from a wadio," he thought, "then that wadio has legs and can move around!"

"Hmmm!" Tweety thought. "Who would want to scare us and send us wunning away into the night?"

Suddenly there was another scream. Tweety flew around the room trying to find where that scream might have come from. He found nothing till . . . he heard a voice call out!

It was **Sylvester**. "I got so scared I had to scream,"
he explained. "I saw a scary bat running about the place."
"Vampires are supposed to become bats at night,"
Tweety thought.

Suddenly, Tweety noticed a piece of paper sticking out of the drawer of a nearby table. The canary gently tugged at the paper till it finally came out. It was a newspaper clipping and what Tweety read astounded him.

"I'm beginning to understand these stwange happenings," Tweety exclaimed. "But why?" He gazed around the room . . . at the staircases, at Sylvester hiding under the bed covers, at the black shoes sticking out from the bottom of the window drapes. **THE SHOES?** Tweety flew over toward them.

Reaching the window, Tweety stuck his head under the drapes. A large black bat peered back at him, just as Sylvester had reported.

"I am Count Crackula, the vampire," he said to Tweety. "And I will harm you all unless you leave at once!"

Tweety handed the clipping to the bat, who read it in tears.

"I am the actor pictured in this review," he cried, removing his mask. "But now I'm a servant to a silly count with bad teeth, who sleeps all day and watches TV at night."

"I hate making breakfast for guests," he explained, "so I scare them away at night. I'd forgotten all about the clipping."

The next day, Granny, Tweety, and Sylvester made their own breakfasts. Granny, who had slept through everything, joined in when she saw Tweety cracking some eggs.

Just before they left, Igor handed Tweety a big bag of cookies to eat for the journey.

"What a nice man," thought Granny. "And not a vampire in sight."